Junior Super Stars

Story by Carmel Reilly
Illustrations by Pat Reynolds

Portland Estates Elementary

Contents

Chapter 1	Go, Eddie!	2
Chapter 2	The Visitor	6
Chapter 3	In the Gym	12
Chapter 4	Brad Chooses	20

Chapter 1

Go, Eddie!

Eddie bounced the ball down the court.
He raced past one player, and then past another.

"Go, Eddie!" yelled Nina.

Within moments, Eddie was at the end of the court.
He threw the ball to Nina
and she passed it back to him.
He took aim at the basket. It was a difficult shot.
The ball slid around the top of the hoop
and fell through.

There were shouts and cheers from the sideline.
Eddie's team had won.

Go, Eddie!

Nina and Eddie returned to their classroom.

"I love playing basketball," said Eddie.
"I wish that I could play it all day."

Nina laughed. "You are a great player, Eddie," she said.

"You're good, too," he said.

"But I'm not nearly as good as you are," said Nina, shaking her head.

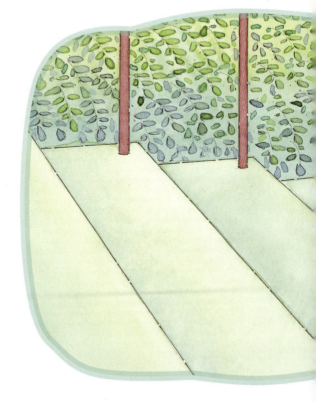

Go, Eddie!

Chapter 2

The Visitor

Mrs Jacobs, the principal,
came into the classroom with a visitor.
"Hello, everybody," she said.
"I'd like to introduce Brad Hill to you.
He is the captain
of the City Super Stars basketball team."

"Brad Hill is fantastic!" Eddie whispered to Nina.
"He's my favourite player. I can't believe he's here!"

"Brad is starting a Junior Super Stars team,"
said Mrs Jacobs.
"He has come to look at our Grades 3 and 4 players."

"Wow!" said Eddie excitedly.
"I'd love to be in that team."

Brad Hill looked around the room and smiled.
"I would like three players from your school
to be in the team," he said.

"The teachers will choose our ten top players,"
Mrs Jacobs explained.
"Their names will be put
on the gym notice board
at lunchtime today."

"I'm going to work with this group tomorrow so that I can select the three best players to be in the Junior Super Stars," said Brad.

The lunchtime bell rang,
and the children quickly put away their books.
"I feel so nervous," said Eddie,
as he and Nina raced across to the gym.

There was already a big group of children standing at the notice board.
"Yahoo!" one of the girls yelled.
"My name's on the list."

Eddie squeezed in between two taller boys.
"Nina! You're in Brad's group, too!" he shouted.
"And so am I!"

The Visitor

Chapter 3

In the Gym

The next morning, Eddie and Nina and the other eight children arrived at school early. Brad was already waiting for them in the gym.

"I'd like to begin with some basic throwing, catching and defending," he said, as they gathered around him. "First, I'll demonstrate some moves with Eddie and Nina."

In the Gym

Brad tried to pass the ball to Nina,
but Eddie leapt between them and grabbed it.

"Nina, you'll need to keep your eye on Eddie,"
said Brad, laughing. "He's very fast."

Brad threw the ball to Nina again.
She moved quickly behind Eddie and snatched it.

In the Gym

Brad nodded. "That's much better," he said. "Now the rest of you can work on those moves, then we'll try something more difficult."

Sometime later, Brad took half of the children
to the end of the court to practise shooting baskets.

Brad threw the ball to Eddie, who caught it,
took aim at the basket, but missed.

He tried again, but the ball spun
around the edge of the hoop
before it fell back towards him.
Eddie was very disappointed with himself.

The children worked hard and fast
for several minutes.

"You five take a break now," Brad shouted,
"while I work with the others."

In the Gym

"I was awful," groaned Eddie.
"I can't believe that I'm playing so badly today."

"Look at Harry. He's shot five baskets already," said Nina. "And Lucy is really fast."

"Everyone is so good.
They're much better than me," said Eddie, with a sigh.
"I don't think I'm going to get into this team."

In the Gym

Chapter 4

Brad Chooses

At home time, Nina, Eddie and the other children returned to the gym.
Brad Hill was going to meet them there
and tell them who was in the team.

"I really want to be in the team,"
Eddie said to Nina,
"but I played so badly this morning,
I'm sure I won't get in."

"It's me who won't get in," said Nina.
"But I know you'll be all right."

Brad Chooses

Brad and Mrs Jacobs arrived.

"First of all," said Brad,
"I have to say that you were all magnificent
and it was very hard to choose three players.
From Grade 4, I have chosen Harry and Lucy."

"Yes!" grinned Harry, giving Lucy, who was sitting nearby, a high five.

"And from Grade 3," said Brad, "I have chosen Eddie."

Eddie leapt into the air with excitement.
"I can't wait for the first game," he said.

"Oh, Eddie!" said Nina.
"I knew you'd get into the team.
I'm going to come along and cheer for you!"